Seth and Beth

Written by
Jenny Phillips

Illustrated by
Alessia Ray

Seth and Beth

BOOK 1

The Big Day

CHALLENGE WORDS

saw

into

their

birds

clouds

heard

they

Chapter 1

This is Seth—a boy with blue eyes, a big smile, and a dog named Gus.

Seth lived in a cute home by a big grove of tall trees called Green Grove.

The home was not big, but it had a big yard that the birds loved.

His dad and mom had a bake shop.

Seth loved to smell the cakes.

In the home next to his lived a girl named Beth. Seth and Beth loved to ride bikes.

One day, Seth and Beth went far into the grove of trees for a picnic.

As they rode their bikes, the birds sang and the sun played in the trees.

They rode their bikes all the way to the big pond. Then, sitting on a big rock, they ate their

lunch—sticks of white cheese and big
red apple tarts from the bake shop.

"This is the best day!"
said Seth.

"Yes, it is!" said Beth.

Seth and Beth played, and then they sat in the shade of a big tree and read books.

They felt the soft breeze on their cheeks, and they felt the warm sun on their legs.

It was not long until they fell fast asleep.

Chapter 2

As Seth and Beth slept, the wind picked up. Dark clouds glided in the sky.

Seth felt a wet plop on his nose. He and Beth woke up. Seth then felt more wet plops.

"Let's go!" yelled Beth.

Just as the children hopped on their bikes, there was a flash in the sky and a big crash.

Beth fell off her bike.

"Oh, my leg!" she said. "I cannot ride my bike."

"I will go get help," said Seth. "Stay here!"

There was too much mud to ride his bike, so

Seth had to run.

Fog rolled into the grove of trees, and it was hard to see.

Seth lost his way. He was wet and scared.

He sat on a rock and prayed.

"God, I need help. Beth fell off her bike and cannot ride, and I am lost. I need to get home."

After some time, Seth heard his dog, Gus, barking.

"Here I am!" yelled Seth.

"Here I am!"

Then, Gus was at Seth's side.

Seth hugged his dog.

Chapter 3

"Take me home!" Seth said to Gus.

Gus and Seth dashed off into the trees.

It was not long until Seth saw his home. Oh, it looked so safe and warm!

Mom and Dad hugged Seth.

"Beth is by the pond," he said. "She fell off her bike.

Can you get her, Dad?"
In a flash, Dad and Gus were on their way to get Beth.

It was not long until Seth's dad came back with Beth. He set her next to the fire.

Seth's mom checked her leg.

"It is not broken. I will call your mom."

Seth said a prayer that night by his bed.

"I am so glad that you helped me and Beth."

He slipped into his bed. The wind still puffed and gusted, but he was snug and safe.

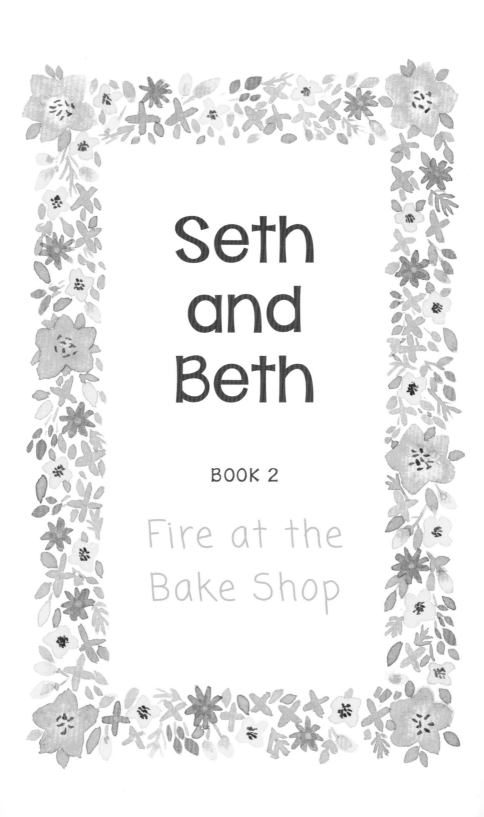

Seth and Beth

BOOK 2

Fire at the
Bake Shop

CHALLENGE WORDS

money

heard

they

Chapter 1

Seth and Gus sat on the back deck of their home. Seth read a book, and Gus slept.

Seth looked up and sniffed. "I smell smoke!" he said.

Just then, he saw smoke coming from his mom and dad's bake shop.

He saw and heard a fire truck zooming up the street.

Seth ran to the bake shop, but he did not get too close.

His mom and dad hugged him. "I left the pot on the stove," said his mom. She felt so bad.

Seth saw the fireman use a big, long hose. It was not long until all the

flames were gone. Most of
the bake shop was saved,
but some of it was not.

The next day, Seth and Beth went to the grove of trees by their homes.

"We have to close the

bake shop," said Seth. "Part of it is black and smells bad. It will cost a lot to fix it."

"Let's help," said Beth.

"How?" asked Seth.

Beth sat on a hard gray rock. "Well, we can sell

apples from my apple tree."

"Let's do it!" said Seth. "Let's go ask your mom."

Plop. Plop. The apples fell into the buckets as Beth and Seth picked.

They picked all day.

"Look," said Beth. "I have ten buckets."

"I have ten buckets, too!" said Seth.

As the sun rose the next day, the kids put the buckets in the back of the blue truck. Beth's

mom drove the truck down the road. Gus sat in the back and loved to feel the wind.

Beth and Seth set up an apple stand. It was a warm day with a soft breeze.

A bird came to see the apples.

"I hope we sell all these buckets," said Beth.

"I will take a bucket," said a man with a green hat as he handed Seth money.

"I will take two buckets," said a girl in a red dress. Beth put the money in a wood box.

Seth and Beth sat at their stand all day. As the sun started to set, a man picked up the last bucket

of apples. "My kids will love these," he said as he handed the kids his money.

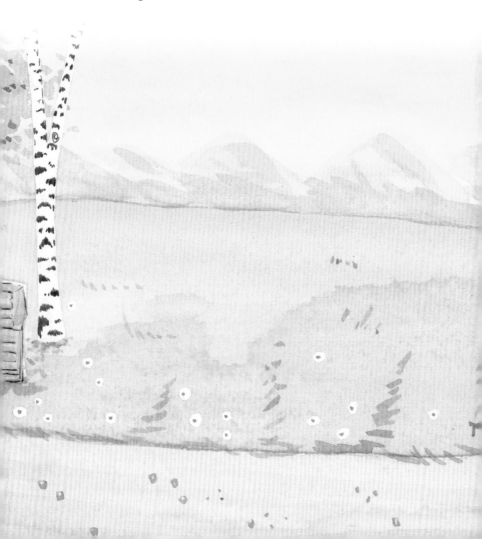

The sun sank into the hills as they drove home in the blue truck.

Seth was so tired. He got in his bed and was asleep in no time.

Chapter 3

The next day, Beth and Seth gave the money to Seth's mom.

She gave them a big, big hug.

Seth went with his dad to the store. They used the money to buy things needed to fix the shop.

Seth helped his dad fix the walls. Gus did not help.

He slept and snored.
In two weeks the shop
was fixed.

Mom baked trays and trays of cakes.

Mom made a tray of cakes just for Beth and Seth.

"Come and see," she said.

Mom took a cloth off the tray. It was filled with small cakes shaped like apples.

Seth bit into his cake. He loved it! He also loved the way he felt.

Helping Mom and Dad fix the bake shop was the best!

Seth
and
Beth

BOOK 3

The Raft

CHALLENGE WORDS

want

friend

clouds

Chapter 1

One day, Beth and Seth rode their bikes to the pond as the clouds drifted in the blue sky.

"Let's make a raft," said Beth.

"Yes!" said Seth.

The kids looked for logs and dragged them into a pile. It was hard to do.

Beth's dad came and gave the kids sacks of lunch.

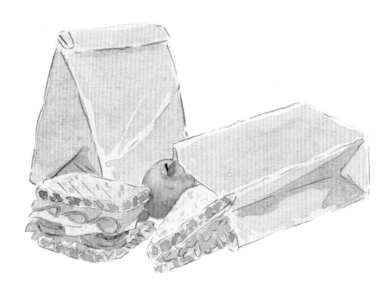

"I will help you," he said. "I will go get my rope."

Beth's dad helped until the raft was finished.

"Let's try it," said Beth.
The kids got on the raft.
It drifted off onto the

pond. Seth used a long
stick to steer the raft. It
was so fun.

The next day, the kids made a red and blue flag for the raft. They swam

all day and played as
the warm sun smiled
on them.

The next day, Beth stopped as she got to the pond.

"Look! Our flag is gone.

There is a black flag on our raft, and there is a young boy that I don't know on the raft."

"This is my raft," said the boy.

"No, it is not," said Seth. "It is our raft."

"You cannot have it," said the boy. "I want it. See, my flag is on it. You cannot have it back."

Seth and Beth were shocked. They went into the grove of trees and made a plan.

"Let's be like Jesus," said Beth.

"Yes," said Seth. "Let's be like Jesus."

They went back to the pond.

"You can have the raft," said Seth. "I am glad you

like it and hope you have fun with it."

"I like your black flag," said Beth.

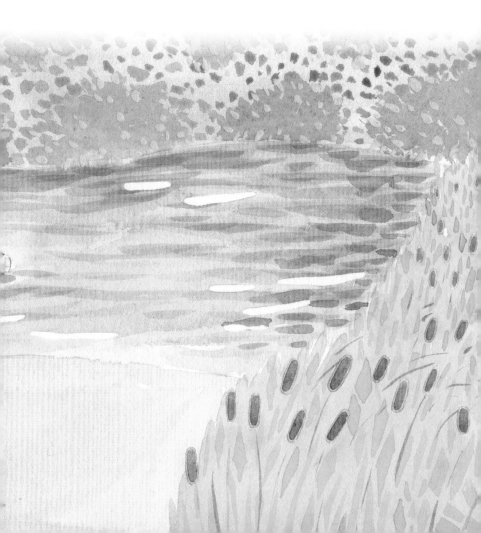

At lunch, the kids gave the boy on the raft some cake.

They smiled at him and asked him to play hide and seek.

They had a lot of fun.

Chapter 3

The next day, Beth and Seth saw the red and

blue flag back on the log raft.

"You can have the raft back," said the boy.

Beth took his black flag and put it on the raft, too.

"We can all have the
raft," she said.
The three friends
cheered.

The End